To my wife, Christin, and our children, Hadley and Baird,
who have been extremely supportive during the making of this book.

I am thankful that I was able to do this project during the COVID-19 pandemic. It happened at a time in my
life when I already had a chance to work all around the north shore of Boston with my job, meet people
from many walks of life, and raise my kids to the ages of 8 and 11. Thanks to all this, it was easy to tell a
story that I would want to illustrate.

And to my nephew, Wesley. My goal was to have this book finished by your birth so you could have a
copy as a gift. Thank you for keeping me motivated!

-JB

Every Friday evening Devante and his family walked to the park, and on their way back they stopped to look at the ducks.

Every week Devante asked his parents
if he could feed the ducks.

And week after week his parents pointed to the signs and said,
"You know we can't, Devante."

Today was going to
be different though.

Devante was
determined to
feed the ducks.

He carefully snuck
some bread from
his dinner plate
into his jacket.

At the park Devante waited for a moment when his parents weren't looking

and then threw the bread into the pond!

All of the ducks swarmed the dinner bread!

Devante hadn't expected the ducks to react so wildly!

"What happened, Devante?" asked his mother.

"The ducks just went crazy! I guess we'll never know why," Devante fibbed.

"Did you feed the ducks?" pressed his mother.

"NO!"
Devante lied again.

He wondered why he couldn't feed the ducks.

The more he thought about it, the angrier he got.

As he dug into his toy box, Devante stewed incredulously, "They tell me I can't feed the ducks?"

"I'm gonna

feed
this
duck!

And as much as I want!"

He started off small
and gave the duck a toy car,
which it gobbled up with delight.

"See! I can feed the ducks!"
Devante said to himself as he searched
for more things to feed it.

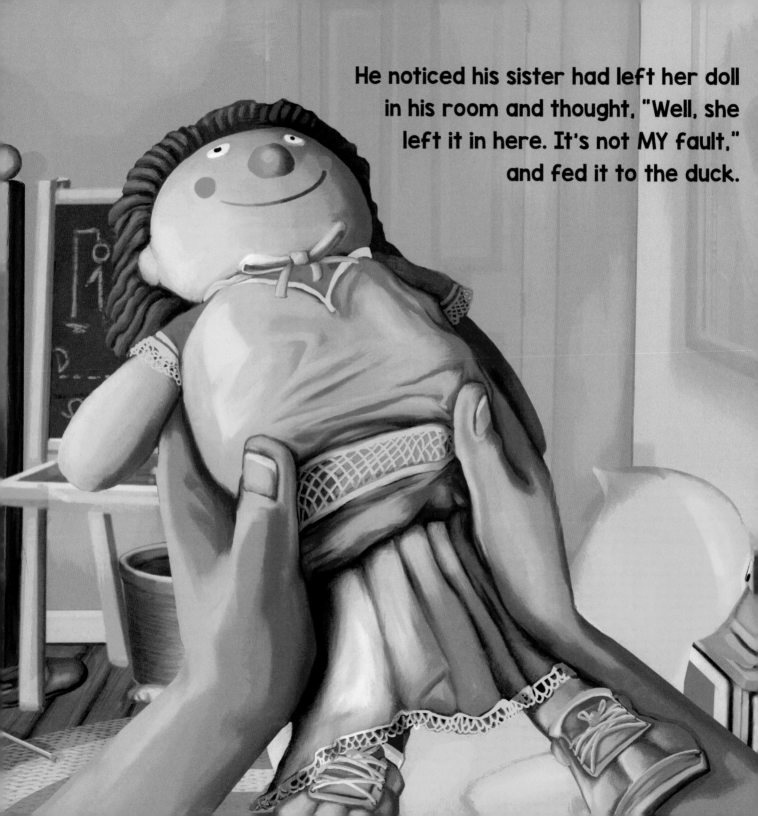

He noticed his sister had left her doll in his room and thought, "Well, she left it in here. It's not MY fault," and fed it to the duck.

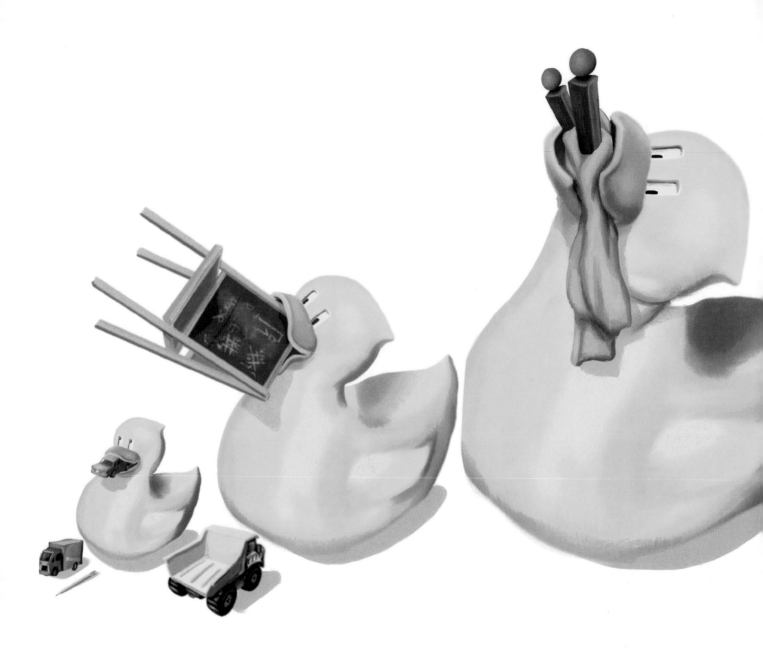

Feeding the duck made Devante feel satisfied,
and he continued to feed it until...

...there was
NOTHING LEFT
in his room to eat.

Devante's parents were watching TV in the living room so Devante snuck the duck past them into the kitchen to look for more things to eat.

Suddenly he heard his parents getting up in the other room. Devante closed all the cabinets and shoved the duck into the pantry. "I'm just getting a snack, Mommy, and then I'll go back to bed," Devante said hurriedly as his mother walked into the kitchen.

"Phew! That was close!" sighed Devante.
Then he noticed everything in the pantry was gone.

"Oh no! You need to stop eating!" exclaimed Devante,

But the duck didn't pay any attention
and just moved
toward the
living room.

"Wait, Duck! Please stop eating everything!" pleaded Devante. The duck seemed to understand him a little but continued eating anyway.

Devante knew he should ask his mom for help
but didn't want to admit what he had done.

His thoughts about solving this problem
himself were interrupted by a

bang

and a

crash

as the duck had finished devouring
everything in the living room and burst
through the wall to outside.

The duck ate bushes, fences, and cars. Then trees, barns, and houses.

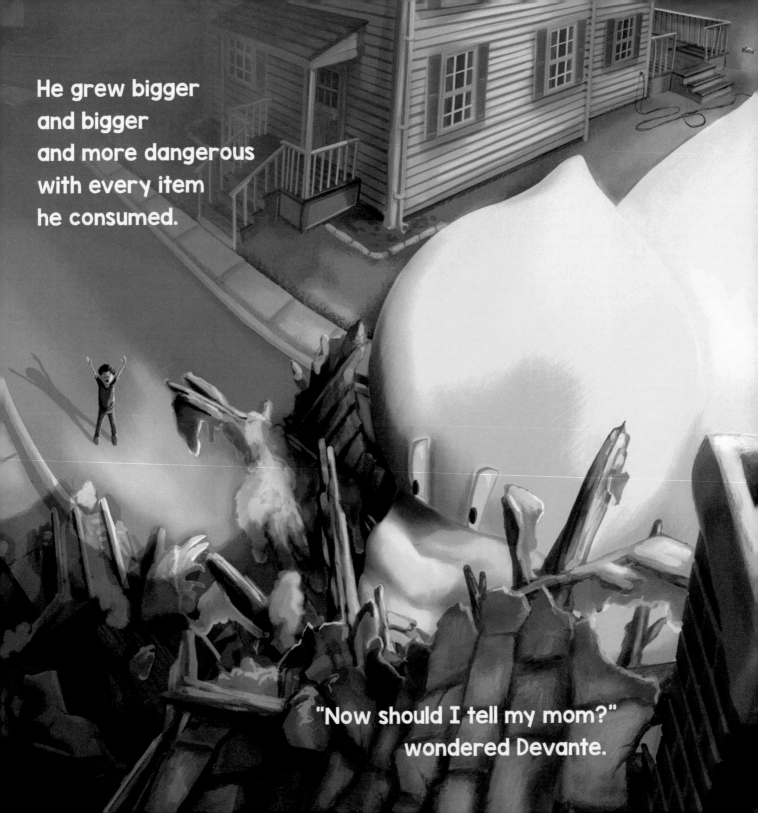

He grew bigger
and bigger
and more dangerous
with every item
he consumed.

"Now should I tell my mom?"
wondered Devante.

Eventually the duck had gotten so big that it began to eat mountains, rivers, and ponds.

Devante realized there was nothing more he could do.

He shouldn't have fed the ducks.

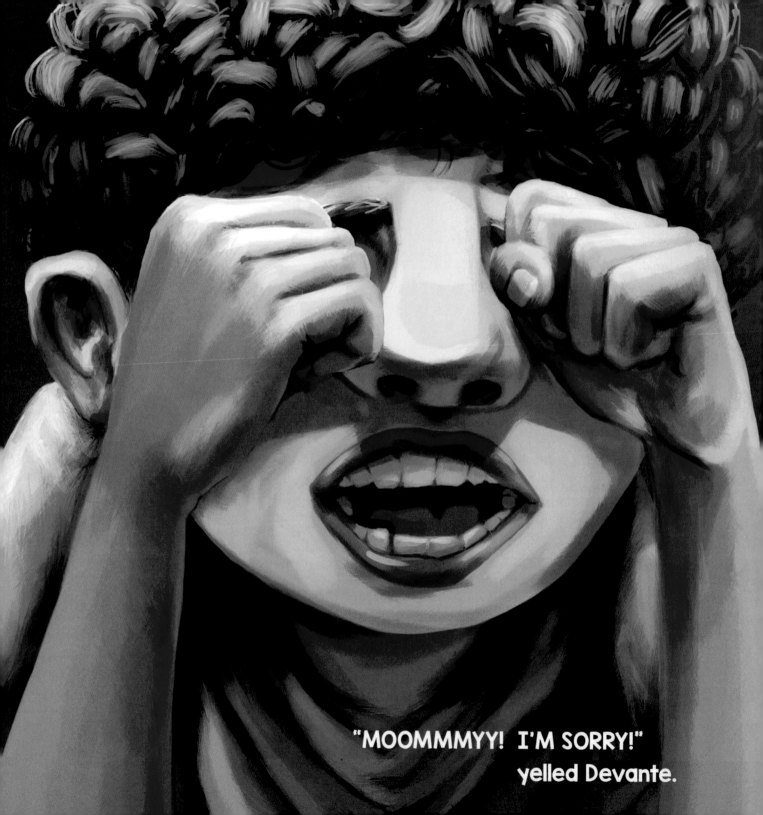

"MOOMMMYY! I'M SORRY!"
yelled Devante.

His mom replied softly, "It's okay, Devante.
I appreciate you telling me that, and I love you very much!
And don't worry; it's not like anything REALLY
bad happened, right?"

Don't Feed The Ducks.

JEREMIAH BROWN spent fifteen years in retail management and left at the end of 2020 to pursue his childhood dream of becoming an illustrator. He grew up in Middleburgh, New York and now lives in Danvers, Massachusetts with his wife, two kids, pet cat and rabbit. He rides his motorcycle whenever it is convenient anytime from spring to fall.

@Jeremiah.BrownIllustration
JeremiahBrownIllustration.com

Coming July 2021!
Join Ayah, Devante's sister,
on an adventure with
monsters and friends!